KANDY KANE ADDICKION

CHRONICLES OF A NYMPHO

AUTHOR LADY LEGACY

LADY LEGACY PRESENTS

This book is dedicated to my loving family, friends, amazing supporters, and my hometown Gadsden, Alabama. I want to encourage anyone with a dream to never be afraid to pursue whatever it is that makes you happy.

Writing books was one of my many dreams, and now it's a dream come true. My message to you is to never give up because you will never fail as long as you are trying to succeed!

My fans; you are the absolute greatest. Thank you for every book you've purchased, read, or reviewed. Your continuous support means everything to me. I have so many storylines coming your way, so be on the lookout.

~Love Your Favorite Indie Author~
AUTHOR LADY LEGACY

SYNOPSIS

At twenty one years old, Kandy Kane is young, and the epitome of beauty. Growing up in a small, town, called Gadsden, Alabama; she had everything she's ever wanted. As the only child, of a notorious Drug Lord; she never wanted for nothing. Unfortunately, everything changed ten years ago, when her father was brutally murdered by his best friend.

Craving her old lifestyle, Kandy started using what she had, to get what she wanted. She knew she'd hit a diamond mine, after one freaky night with Dr. Nikolas Kane, he proposed the very next day. The doctor thought it was love at first sight; but in reality he was pu**sy whipped at first stroke.

Sadly, he knows nothing about his new promiscuous wife, other than her striking features and mind-blowing sex. Little does he know, Kandy is an undercover FREAK, AND A NYMPHO! Can you turn a hoe into a housewife? Get ready to experience treachery, pain, rage, and revenge like you've never seen before in a story called, "ADDICKION."

INTRODUCTION

Let me properly introduce myself. My name is Kandy Kane. Yeah, you heard me right. It's my real name, no lie. That shit sounds sweet, and sexy as fuck. I still gotta get used to my new legal name myself. I used to be Kandy O'Neil. I know that shit sounds BOR-ING... riggghht! Anyway, I recently got married, and I can thank Dr. Nikolas Kane for giving my full name that sexy ass twist. He calls me his candied cane. I'm sure I taste like one.

I'm young as hell. I'm only twenty-one years old, and my husband is twenty years my senior. Mmmm hmmm; he's forty-one years old. You added it up right. Dude dick game is straight garbage, but his oral is banging. I remember the first time we fucked. I fucked him so good dude proposed they very next day. True story ya'll. Was I supposed to turn down his proposal? Hell, nah! I ain't dumb by a long shot. Who in their right mind would turn down a successful dentist? Not I... not Kandy!

My husband is a sexy Italian. Well I say Italian, other people say he's white; but trust me, forty-one looks good on him. Truth be told, Nikolas doesn't look a day older than thirty years old. I LOVE being a dentist's wife. I get to live a luxurious life; and as long as I keep his stomach full and his balls empty, he's satisfied.

As for me, I'm never satisfied. I can never get enough of sex. I'm a sex addict. Ssshh! Don't tell anyone my dirty secret. My poor husband doesn't have a clue. I've been fucking since I was eleven years old, but that shit wasn't by choice. That's another long ass story.

Sex for me is like a dope to a fiend. So… me being faithful is out of the question. I pounce on dick for pleasure, not love. Many of you might asked me, why did I get married? Damn, I guess you slow or something. A bitch needs financial stability; and Nikolas is a sucker for love, or maybe young pussy. Shit, I really don't care how no one feels, because we both getting what the hell we want.

I fuck on impulse, to get my next high. It's nothing personal, so please don't catch feelings. I constantly need dick, and I can't explain why. Call me the new age Janet Jackson. I know you remember her freaky song… "Anytime, Anyplace." Yeah, that's me all day every day. I'm a fucking NYMPHO, and I don't give two fucks what you think. Just sit back and relax. I got a story to tell. Welcome to my world of ADDICKION!!!

~ Kandy Kane ~

CHAPTER ONE

"HURRY THE HELL UP"

Kandy

I was hotter than a pot of boiling grits. Nikolas' horny, limp dick ass had woken me up out of my sleep. He wanted some pussy to go. You know, pussy before you go to work. I had my legs spread wide; while he tried to insert his semi hard dick inside me. It was quite annoying, and it was a pitiful attempt to say the least.

"I wish he would just hurry the hell up. With all the money he has, you would think he would go, and buy himself a new dick."

"Spread your legs wider." Nikolas said frustrated.

"Are you serious? If I spread my legs any wider they might as well detach from my body." I spat angrily.

"Hold still baby. I'm almost fully erected." Nikolas said, probing his soft meat against my slit. I rolled my eyes, wishing he would hurry the hell up.

"He wasn't getting nowhere, no time soon."

"Why don't you write yourself a prescription for Viagra?" I

asked irritated. I knew that would piss him off, and I could care less. An instant scowl appeared on Nikolas' handsome face.

"Kandy, I don't need no fucking Viagra; and you know damn well I would never do such a thing. Have you ever heard of a dentist writing a prescription for Viagra? Stop being sarcastic!" he snapped, looking at me with a disapproving face. I almost burst out to laughing, but I held my composure.

"Order some samples offline or something. Whether you want to admit it or not, you have a problem Nikolas. Just go down on me already." I said, pleading for his oral and not asking.

"I bet this tongue will shut your complaining ass up," he mumbled under his breath.

He repositioned himself so he could eat me out. Nikolas hooked his forearms around my slender brown thighs. He stuck his lengthy tongue out to full capacity, then began dipping his snakelike tongue in and out of my slit. I can't lie, my husband's head game is the truth. It was no doubt an electrifying pleasure. Immediately I let out a low, deep moan.

"Damn, it feels so GOOD! His tongue by far is the most useful tool on his body."

"Hmmm. Your pussy so sweet baby." Nikolas said in a muffled tone. He continued licking and viciously eating me out.

"Yes, I know its sweet... now keep going baby." I lifted my small hips, smashing my pussy against his pointed nose. Nikolas oral skills had me feeling exhilarated. It was feeling so damn good I had no choice, but to succumb to his elongated tongue.

Nikolas unlocked his right forearm from my thigh and wrapped his hand around his inflating dick. He started a slow ejaculation while he was eating my pussy. I'm pretty sure he was getting REAL hard by now. I don't know why, but every time he ate my candy box his dick would always get harder.

"Maybe I should bottle up my juices. It seems to be the cure to

erectile dysfunction." I thought, with a mischievous smile.

I guess he felt like it was time to give his erected dick a second chance. Without warning Nikolas popped his seven inches into my slippery mound. He humped madly like a wild animal. It was the most aggressive ten pumps ever. Then the next thing I know he was nutting all inside me.

"Damn it Nikolas. All I needed was twenty more aggressive pumps and his old ass couldn't even pull that off." I silently fumed. I reckon he was satisfied, because I sure hell wasn't.

He jumps out of bed and kisses me on the cheek.

"Love you baby. I gotta get to work." he said. Then he runs off to take a quick shower.

"Love me my ass."

I was mad as hell all over again. Just when I was about to cum, he ups and beats me to the punch. Then he has the nerve to dip on me.

"How the fuck he gone get his nut and leave unfinished business? Oh, you got yours, best believe I'm getting mines."

Nikolas stepped out the bathroom wearing his custom black slacks and a casual white button down. His shirt was half buttoned. He proceeds to finish buttoning up his Tommy Hilfiger shirt and looks through his ties with a look of uncertainty. I can tell he didn't know which tie he wanted to wear. He held two ties up in the air. One was red and the other one was grey.

"Here comes the question." I thought.

"Baby which tie should I wear?" he asked skeptically.

"The blue one." I said being funny as fuck. I knew blue wasn't one of the damn choices. I didn't give damn which tie he wore as long as he got the hell on. He needed to go so I can fix his fuck up. I'm horny, and I'm in my damn feelings.

"Oh, don't be like that my little Candied Cane. I guess I'll wear the red tie," he said with a smirk, winking his eye.

Nikolas puts on the red tie, grabs his white lab coat and headed out the bedroom.

"I'll call you later when I get a break!" I heard him yelling before walking out the front door.

"I plan on ignoring him, just the way he ignored my needs. I swear he works my last nerves."

Nikolas leaves the house faithfully around 7:00 a.m. every morning. He normally gets to the office around 7:30 a.m. since the dental office opened at 8:00 a.m. I thought about hitting up one of my side pieces, but hell, it was too damn early. I figured I could go back to sleep for a couple hours and get my nut later. Then again, I figured I should go ahead and get my orgasm out of the way.

"Let me get this quick fix."

I got out of bed and searched inside my sex toy drawer. I found the perfect plastic dick. He has no problem hitting my G-Spot. I call him Mr. Chocolate. He's twelve inches long, has a rotating head, and ten different functions.

I lubed myself up and rammed the plastic dick inside my pussy over and over again. I had the dick head rotating like the exorcist, and the speed was on ten. It was like having hardcore sex with ya damn self. By the time I was done, nut was running all over my hands and the toy.

"Hmmm; just what I needed. If you want something done right, do it your damn self." I thought with a gratified smile, lying back down to catch so more zzz's.

CHAPTER TWO

"THUG LOVE"

Kandy

L ying in bed, I realized its 11:00 a.m. and I can't sleep peacefully. Nikolas' whipped ass keeps calling me every hour on the hour. I was ready to get up anyway. I needed to take a hot shower.

"Ain't no use of wasting a beautiful summer day."

Slinging my tone legs over the side of my queen size Venus bed, I walked sluggishly into the bathroom. I started a hot shower and stepped in, letting the hot water bead against my chocolate skin. I grabbed my Summer Eve's Intimate Wash, squirted a few drops on my loofa, and washed up.

The instant I got out the shower and dried off, my phone started to ring. I was huffing and puffing, stomping all the way to my bedroom to grab my phone. I had a whole attitude. I just knew it was Nikolas calling me for the umpteenth time. A smile slowly crept across my face when I realized it was my boo Quincy.

Quincy was a dude closer to my age. He was twenty-five years old, and a Northside drug dealer doing decent for himself. He was kinda on the chubby side, but he fulfilled a lot of my sexual cravings. The good thing about Quincy was, we had fun sex with no strings attached.I plopped my bare ass on the edge of the bed and quickly slid my index finger across the phone screen.

"Hello Q." I said, batting my long eyelashes.

"What it do sexy? You gonna roll through today or not?" he asked, getting straight to the point.

"I guess I have a lil time to play. Where you at?" I asked, holding the phone in the crook of my neck while applying Pink Chiffon body cream to my legs.

"I'm in the trap, but you can meet at the Crown in bout thirty." he responded. Crown is a gas station in the hood everyone kinda hung out at. It's like a one stop shop.

"Alright Q. See you in about thirty minutes." I said, rushing him off the phone.

I finished lotioning up and got dressed. I threw on some short khaki shorts, a yellow tank and my Michael Kor flip flops. Even though I didn't have a big ass, it was just right. My titties weren't big either, but I was satisfied with my B cups. Once I got dressed, I stepped back in the bathroom. Grabbing a rat tail comb, I put my natural, curly hair in a low sleek bun and fleeked my edges down with a small toothbrush.

"This Eco Gel is the truth when it comes to your edges."

"Okay bitch, you cute." I said out loud while looking into the mirror. I was pleased at the image staring back at me.

I sashayed out the bathroom, grabbed my Michael Kors crossbody, and headed out the door, jumping into my 2018 red Camaro SS. That V8 was a beautiful beast. It had all that horsepower; reminding me of myself. I absolutely love the rush, and the pure adrenaline I got whenever I drove it. My tag was also cute. It read, 4KandyK. It was a gift from my husband of course.

My phone rang again. I was heading to the Crown store off Tuscaloosa Avenue to meet Q. After I noticed it was Nikolas, I decided to answer this time. I pushed his buttons a little, but I didn't want him leaving work looking for me.

"Hello Nikolas." I said, dipping through traffic.

"Kandy, where you been all day? I've called you every hour since I left going to work this morning," he said sounding upset.

"I was just getting ready to call you back. I actually went back to sleep after you left. I'm just getting up."

"Oh. For minute I was getting worried. I almost left work to see if you were okay." he said, sounding relieved that I had answered.

"I'm good baby. There's no need to leave work."

"I could actually meet you for lunch. Let' do lunch at Top O' the River," he suggested sounding all cheerful.

"Damn. What the fuck can I say? I'm on my way to meet Q." I thought, trying my best to think of a smooth lie.

"Baby we can go later. I promised Chassidy we would go shopping. I was actually heading her way to scoop her up." I lied.

"You know I don't like Chassidy. She's a bad influence on you. I wish you would cut your ties of her completely," he said in a condescending tone.

"If he only knew." I said to myself.

"Listen Nikolas, I'm not having this conversation with you. I'll see you when you get off. BYE!!!" I said agitated, ending the call.

"I don't have time to listen to him talk down on Chassidy. I'll end my marriage before I end my five friendship with my best friend. Nikolas is an awesome sugar daddy, but he's replaceable!"

I pulled up at the Crown store. There were plenty of niggas hanging out, thots; and a few dope fiends were getting served. I looked around for Q. He was handling his business, so I decided to wait inside the car until he finished. Once he spotted my car he was all smiles. He quickly served the fiend, then after the exchange, started walking in my direction. Q had on some sagging black Levi's, white Air Force Ones, a wife-beater, and a long platinum chain with the letter Q.

"Where you wanna go shawty?" he asked, showing off his opened face, diamond cut grill.

"Let's go to Lookout Mountain." I said, horny as hell.

"Bet. Let's hit that bitch up. Follow me, I don't want to get ya married ass in trouble." he said, laughing as he walked towards his black Caddy.

"He got jokes. He better be glad I love his dick, or I would have burnt tire tracks in his laughing face."

Q is real cute to be chubby. I've told him a million times he looks like the rapper Twista. These girls in Gadsden be on his ass, but Q ain't the type to settle down. Truth be told, I ain't the type to settle down either; but I be damn if I spend the rest of my life in the projects like my mother.

I followed Q to Lookout Mountain. He pulled in and I parked right beside him. We both stepped out the car, and we embraced pelvis to pelvis. He hugged my ass so tight I could tell he definitely missed me. I mean, his dick was literally poking me through his jeans.

"Let's get busy baby. Time is money sexy." Q said, adjusting the back seat of his caddy. He knew we had to have plenty of room to get our freak on. I also knew he had to get back to his hustling, so we had to make this quick.

Lookout Mountain is a common spot people frequently went to fuck, smoke, or just relax. It oversees the small city of Gadsden, and the police doesn't ride up there often. It's the perfect getaway spot.

Q ended up fucking my ass so good in the back seat of the Caddy, he had me dreading it was over. That's that thug love. It's different from fucking a square like Nikolas. Every hole on my body is sore, but I was satisfied in every way possible.

"Damn shawty. You got you got that CBP (come back pussy). If I was the wifing up type you would be at the top of my list." Q said as sweat dripped profusely off his chubby face.

"Aww. That's sweet to know Q. I'll get atcha later sexy. Cash App me my money" I said, stepping out the caddy.

"I got you. I just sent you a rack."

"Thank you love."

I blew Q a kiss and left him in his thoughts. I jumped in my Camaro and called up my girl Chassidy.

CHAPTER THREE

"CHASSIDY CONFESSION"

Kandy

R ing, Ring, Ring.

"Hey bestie." Chassidy answered.

"Heifer, what took you so long to answer the phone?"

"Girl, I had to kick Ahmad out my damn apartment."

"Why you keep fucking with him Chassidy?" I snapped.

"Girl I don't know. Everybody ain't able to land a dentist with money. You living the good life in the Country Club; but I still got bills that need to be paid." she said, with a trace of jealousy.

Chassidy is known for having a pity party and throwing tantrums. I overlook her crazy ass, because if she want better than hell, do better. I don't feel sorry for her, but I love her nonetheless.

"Bills... Bitch, I know you don't call that Section 8 apartment bills. Hell, your apartment is based off your fucking income

Chassidy. Anyhoo, I told Nikolas I was hooking up with you, so I'm on my way over there." I said, agitated with my bestie.

"Okay Kandy, see you in a lil bit." she said then hung up the phone.

"Heifer." I thought.

Chassidy is nineteen years old, redbone, average height, and her body is built like an hour glass. She is often mistaken as the oldest when we're together because of how well developed she is. Chassidy's teeth are kinda big for her mouth. She has that Gina from Martin thing going on. I figured she must have needed braces as a kid, but it doesn't take away from her natural beauty. Then she keeps her hair and nails on fleek.

We've been friends for the past five years. In fact, she was at the club when I first met Nikolas. I haven't been married that long, and Chassidy been in her funky ass feelings ever since I got with Nikolas. It's cool though. If she leaves Ahmad alone and get out of messy ass River Hill Apartments, she'd be good.

"Hell, she need to land herself a real baller." I said to myself. I'm fortunate my husband is a dentist. I don't know one twenty-one-year-old living the life I live.

I grew up in Myrtlewood projects. Some people call them Myrtlewood; but to anyone who's ever lived there, we called them hoes Murdawood. My mom is the project hairstylist. She did the best styles in town, minus the high-end prices. It seems no matter how hard she hustled, she could never make enough money to leave the projects. I even offered to help, but she declined. That shit is fucked up, because her ass is still in the projects hustling. It's not like she has to be there, but to each their own.

We ain't always lived in the projects. After my father was murdered, we had no choice. We went from middle class to lower class in a blink of an eye. It was the most heartbreaking moments of my life. I'm glad I'm finally back on the map financially. I was a little girl when my father died, but I was determined to get back to the top. I used my looks to get me where I am today. I knew once I got the first opportunity I was out them messy ass projects. Then when I met Nikolas, I knew he was that meal ticket.

Reminiscing

I met Nikolas at this club called Lucy's Afterlife. It's a club in the heart of downtown Gadsden. The crowd is mixed, and I was there one Saturday night with my girl Chassidy. Chassidy and I had walked to the bar to get some drinks. Nikolas stood out at the bar. He was tall, mysterious, and handsome. I was definitely intrigued. There were a couple of thots surrounding him. I could tell they were thirsty, which meant he had that paper. He was dressed like he owned the damn club, and he smelled delicious.

Anyhoo, I walked my hot ass up to the bar with my bestie. I leaned over the bar, making sure he got an eyeful of my small ass. I had on a short black dress, laced thongs, some fake red bottoms and a fake Louie bag. Shit looked real though. I knew a glimpse of my ass would catch his attention. I pretended to buy my own drink, and that's when he offered to pay. The rest is history. We've been together ever since.

I was happy as hell to learn he was a dentist that owned his own practice. Then when I found out he was living large in Gadsden's Country Club. I knew at that moment he was my way out the Westside projects. So hell yeah we fucked after the club. I use my young pussy to whip his old ass, and it worked.

I giggled, reminiscing at the lengths I took to get Nikolas.

'A bitch was determined!'

My engine roared as I pulled up at Chassidy's one-bedroom apartment. I parked my car out front and walked to her door, knocking a few times before she answered.

"Hey bestie. Sorry about earlier; I was in my feelings," she said looking sad.

"You think? But... it's cool. I understand. Ahmad is a jerk, and he doesn't deserve you. Hold the fuck up... Did that nigga bust your lip Chassidy? Were ya'll fighting?" I spat.

"Girl yes, and yes. I confronted him about messing around with Brittney from the eastside, and he went ballistic. I'm straight. He hits like a bitch. I'm just happy he gave me $300 for my bills," she said unbothered.

"Ahmad needs his ass whooped. I don't give a damn about him paying your bills. I'm concerned he had the fucking balls to touch you. Hell, I could have given you $300 Chassidy," I said pissed off.

"She shoulda called the police on his weak ass."

"Well, I didn't want to take your money Kandy. Then, you know your husband can't stand me for whatever reason. So, I humbly decline," she spat.

"Let me worry about Nikolas. Go fix your face, I'm about to take your ass shopping," I said popping her big ass. It jingled like a bowl of Jell-O.

"Aww, Kandy! I love you chick."

"I love you more Chassidy."

"No, I'm secretly in love with you Kandy. That's why Nikolas, and I can't stand each other. I think he knows." she said, fingering through her burgundy faux locs.

"Girl, you tripping. You can't be..." I tried to say, but Chassidy leaned in for a kiss. She has always had bisexual tendencies, but we have never been intimate.

"Damn her lips were sweet like cherries." I thought.

She leans again grabbing my little ass and pushes her tongue deeper inside my mouth this time. We stood locking tongues for a few moments before she starts guiding me towards her bedroom.

"Damn I felt a fire unleash within me. What the fuck is this feeling? I've never felt this shit before." I thought.

I allowed my bestie to walk me inside her bedroom. Chassidy gently laid me down on her bed. I should have stopped her, knowing damn well Q and I just fucked, but I couldn't form the words. It was like I was in a sexual trance. She undressed me slowly, kissing every inch of my slender body. I let out a soft moan with each kiss. My slit was glistening from the puddle forming between my legs.

"Lay right there." Chassidy instructed, stepping out of her clothes. Her body was beautiful. Her big red titties, her curvy hips, and her plump ass. She had a fresh Brazilian wax, and her pussy hair was shaped in a cute little heart.

Once my bestie was completely undressed, Chassidy went down on me. She started tonguing my pussy in the same method of how she kissed me.

"Oh my God this shit feels so amazing."

My pedicured toes were balled up, and my face was distorted. My eyes were rolling up in my head. My soft moans were starting to get louder. Biting my bottom lip gently, I was trying to contain the scream that was threatening to escape my mouth. I felt an unfamiliar pleasure, and it felt good as fuck. Never in my life have I been pleased by female.

"Damn I've been missing out."

Just when I thought it was over with, Chassidy turned it up a notch. She opened my legs wider. Then she slid her soft mound in between my legs. I guess this is what lesbian lovers call scissoring. Our clits were humping and grinding in a circular motion; our juices mixing and sliding against our lips. Chassidy was working my shit REAL good. I couldn't stop her if I wanted too.

"This bitch is a pussy grinding pro." I thought.

"Damn Chassidy, you got me ready to cum."

"I got something else I wanna try," she cooed.

Chassidy slid from between my legs. She went to the top drawer of her chest. Just when I thought I've seen it all, this heifer pulls out a strap on dick.

"Chassidy has more secrets than a damn call girl."

She quickly straps on her plastic dick, and orders me to get into doggy style position. I complied out of curiosity. I wanted to know if she could fuck me like a real nigga with that dick.

Chassidy oiled the plastic dick up and fucked the dog shit out of me. I mean I was screaming and bucking like a born-again virgin. I think I might have cum four times, by the time it was over.

My knees had buckled from the last orgasm and I flopped breathless into the bed. I was tired as fuck and Chassidy had did all the damn work. I can't believe my bestie just fucked me. Then the surprising part is, I can't believe I enjoyed it.

"Whew, I guess there's no time to go shopping," I said with a light chuckle. "I gotta get home bestie."

I was completely exhausted. I rolled over and grabbed my phone. I had three missed calls from Nikolas, so I jumped up and started getting dressed.

"Yeah. Call me later Kandy." Chassidy said, looking disappointed.

I kissed Chassidy tenderly on her full lips. "Cheer up bestie. I enjoyed the sex. Who knows, I might let you have a round two soon." I said with a sly smile, biting my bottom lip flirtatiously.

A broad smile appeared upon her pretty face. She walked me to the door, we said our goodbyes and I went home to limp sausage. I couldn't believe how fast the day flew by.

"I'm going to get Nikolas some Viagra one way or another. I might need to hit Q up later." I thought, speeding down Rainbow Drive, heading home.

CHAPTER FOUR

"DINNER DATE"

Nikolas

I t's Saturday evening and yesterday was my last day of work. I'm happy my work week has finally ended. It was a long, exhausting week at the office. All I want to do is spend a nice, romantic night with my beautiful wife.

My family hates the fact I married a black woman, and to know she's only twenty-one baffles them. We didn't have the traditional wedding. We eloped and had a shotgun wedding in Vegas. I proposed the next day after we had AMAZING sex.

I know it sounds like a drastic, irrational decision, but it doesn't matter what my family thinks. It doesn't matter what my friends think. Kandy is the love of my life. Even though Kandy is my first interracial relationship, she's not the first black female I've slept with.

I've always had a fascination with the sex appeal of a black woman. Love has no color in my eye sight, but my family thinks otherwise. They felt I should have married a nice white doctor, lawyer, or just a white woman period. They're just stuck in their old racist ways; but it's their problem, not mines.

My family hardly speaks to me, and my neighbors be side eying me. They look at Kandy like she's the black plague that has contaminated their perfect community, but she speaks even if they don't speak back. The Country Club is our home, and I work just as hard as anyone else. If they got a problem with my wife, they can ALL move for all I care. As far as the Kane family... we are here to stay!

"Kandy are you almost ready my love?" I shouted toward our master bathroom.

"Yes, I'm almost ready. Be right out Nikolas."

"Okay, I'm starving. I can't wait to get to Top O' The River."

"I'm hungry too. You been craving Top O' The River all week. I'm almost done, just touching up my makeup." Kandy yelled out.

I love Top O' The River. I'm happy we're finally going, since Kandy turned down lunch earlier this week. Top O' The River is a well-known, family owned, catfish and seafood restaurant located off Coosa River in Gadsden, Alabama. The restaurant normally stays extremely busy, but never to too busy for me. I made our reservation for six p.m. I'm good friends with the owner's family, so luckily I can always get a table.

Kandy finally stepped out the bathroom wearing a red, form fitting dress with a split up her right leg. She looks breath taking, and I'm very lucky to have someone of her caliber. Kandy is super model quality, and she's all mines.

My milk chocolate Candied Cane is GORGEOUS. Kandy is about 5'7 in height, size eight but very curvy. She weighs approximately 135 pounds, has a slender body, and she has the most toned legs I've ever seen. Her body is banging, and her sex is better than anyone I've EVER been with. She's young, but she knows how to please a man!

"All ready." Kandy coos, twisting around in her authentic red bottoms.

"You look astonishing my love. Let's go."

Once we got to my car, I opened the passenger's door to my 2018 silver Jaguar XJ. I allowed my wife to get settled in then closed her door and hopped in the driver's seat.

It only took about seven minutes to get to the restaurant from the house. I enjoy our date nights. We go out every Saturday. I couldn't have my twenty-one-year-old wife getting bored with me. I try my best to keep her entertained and happy. It just so happens we have a lot in common despite the age difference. We both love to eat, we both love to party, and we both LOVE SEX!

"Match made in heaven."

I parked my car and got out to open Kandy's door. We walked hand in hand into the restaurant. I could feel the stares and hear some whispers, but it didn't bother me. We walked past all the hungry people that were waiting to be called for seating. I said my name to the hostess, and we were immediately seated.

The food was delicious as always. The catfish, collard greens, coleslaw, onions and cornbread were perfect. Kandy and I were so full we had no room for dessert. Kandy normally takes some Macadamia Nut Cheese Cake to go, but she declined desert this time. I generously tipped the waitress, and now it was time to party. As we were leaving out the restaurant a tall, light complected guy spoke to Kandy without as much acknowledging my presence.

"What's up Kandy?" he said walking past us. I could have sworn the guy mean mugged me, but it might have been in my head. I tend to get very protective and jealous when it came to Kandy.

"Hey Marco." Kandy speaks dryly, with a slight wave of her

hand. I could sense some nervousness in her voice, but we kept walking towards my car. I didn't like to make scenes; however, I will be questioning her about Marco as soon as she get inside the car.

We finally made it to the car, I opened her door as normal. She stepped inside the Jag and I slammed her door shut in anger. I hurriedly walked to my side, opened my door, flopped into my seat and slammed my door shut as well. I was fuming with jealousy and rage.

"What the fuck is your problem Nikolas?" she snaps with major attitude.

"Are you fucking serious Kandy? You just spoke to a man without acknowledging me as your husband. Then your friend was mean mugging me. Do you know how that makes me feel? You didn't utter a fucking word; and who the hell is Marco? Are you cheating on me?" I asked with venom dripping off my tongue.

Just the thought of Kandy cheating drove me insane.

"Of course I'm not cheating. Nikolas, that's just ridiculous. I have everything I want. I have no need to cheat. I'm young, but not dumb. Marco went to Gadsden City High with me. Maybe he had a lil high school crush on me. End of discussion." she said, rolling her eyes and looking away from me.

She crossed her long, sexy legs, turning her head towards the passenger window. I could tell she was upset with me. Even though I lost my cool, I couldn't stand my wife being upset with me. I had to smooth things over.

"I'm sorry Kandy. Forget we had this conversation. Let's just enjoy the rest of the night." I said, swallowing my pride.

I grabbed her small chin and turned it towards me before I kissed her very passionately. Our tongues were dipping in and out of each other's mouth before she paused.

"Oh baby! Your tongue is tasting like catfish. We both can

use some Altoids, Double Mint gum, Certs or something," she laughed out hysterically.

"Fair enough baby. You got jokes I see. Look in the glove compartment; I keep some Listerine strips on standby." I laughed out, forgetting all about the argument.

CHAPTER FIVE

"LUCY'S AFTERLIFE CLUB"

Kandy

I was happy the argument with Nikolas ended in the car. Of course I knew who Marco was. Marco was a nigga in his feelings. He was mad because I stopped fucking with him; and that's because his bitch went through his phone. Marco's girlfriend found our dirty lil text messages and started blowing me up. I had to block that hoe. Hell, I didn't want her man, just his dick every once in a while; but now, I don't want shit from him.

That drama happened two weeks ago. Today was the first day I saw him since I cut him off. I believe that nigga is suspect. A down low nigga. The only thing he ever wanted to do was hardcore anal. He never, ever fucked my pussy. That shit was strange, but he always paid big, so I allowed him to do his thang. Then he always made me cum, so it was a plus.

I really wanted to cuss Marco out, but I knew I couldn't do that shit in front of Nikolas. Hell, Marco so damn bitter that nigga probably would have exposed me right inside the restaurant. I couldn't take the risk.

After we left the restaurant parking lot, we went downtown to Lucy's Afterlife. It was the club where me and Nikolas originally met. The crowd was thick to be such a small club. The music was banging, and I couldn't wait to dance and grind all over Nikolas' dick. I love flossing my man in bitches' faces.

The DJ was playing, 'Back That Azz Up' by Juvenile. That's one song that never got old in my book, even though it first came out in 1998. That shit over twenty years old and still can turn the club out. If I had some liquor in me, I would have hit the dance floor on that song.

The white girls were wilding on the dance floor. They were dancing all over each other to a rhythm only they could hear. That shit was funny as fuck, but at least they were having fun. The black girls were dancing like professional strippers, and some were just doing way too much.

Some females had bad weaves, bad hair color and old braids. Then some females were sexy as hell and conceited as fuck. Hell, this club was our spot. I love the variety. Everyone was having fun and that's what partying is all about.

Nikolas looked sexy as hell. His dark hair was combed to the back, and his goatee was thick, sexy, and lined to perfection. He had on white pants, a fitted white tee, and a light blue short sleeved shirt with some casual dark brown loafers.

My husband was GQ smooth, and he was very much in shape. Nikolas wasn't real muscular, but he was naturally toned. He had more of an athletic physique. He had a swag about him that drew all women to him. Hell, ANY man that had a professional career like Nikolas could get the panties in this small town. Just about everybody knew he was a dentist. I love how he stayed true to himself. Even though he was married to a black female, Nikolas never changed who he was.

All eyes were on us. We walked towards the bar, to grab a few drinks before hitting the dance floor. He leaned over yelling over the music, "What would you like to drink?" I was in a zone for a moment. His teeth was so white and perfectly aligned he could make a Crest commercial.

"Did you hear me baby?" He asked once again.

"Oh, I'm sorry. Let me get a double shot of Hen and Coke." I said out loud to Nikolas.

"Okay babe."

"Let me have a double shot of Hen and Coke, and a double shot of Jack Daniels and Coke." Nikolas said to the thirsty blond bartender.

"She can look all she wants, but if she gets out of pocket I'm jumping over this damn bar at her fat ass!" I silently fumed.

I know I got a damn nerve with all my skeletons in my closet, but I still didn't play over Nikolas. I worked too damn hard to get in my position, and I be damn if I give it up for ANYBODY. Besides... I love Nikolas. I just don't love his dick; but I got a plan to fix that shit.

I'm going to holla at Q. I'm sure he has the blue pills I need to help Nikolas. Q is a real hustla. He serves dope, pills, syrup; you name it. If Nikolas refuses to handle his problem, I will do it for him. If I have to sneak that shit in him he's going to fuck me right for once.

After going through a few drinks at the bar, Nikolas and I were ready to hit the dance floor. We normally provided the club with an intimate show. Most people are shocked to know Nikolas ass can actually dance.

"Are you ready my love?" Nikolas asked with low, sexy eyes. I could tell he was horny, but his problem downstairs can't handle me for real. I ignored those sexy, beautiful eyes and slid through the crowd to get our dance on.

"Yes, I'm ready boo. Let's show these people how to dance." I bragged, bouncing to the dance floor. I swerved my tiny hips from side to side and Nikolas followed close behind.

By now the DJ had started playing some throwback Reggae. It was on and popping now. One thing about Nikolas, he was so versatile. He loved all music... even REGGAE! 'Every One Falls In Love' by Devontae and Tanto Metro had everyone in straight heat. It was a lot of sweating, grinding, gyrating, kissing, poking and groping. There was no doubt in my head somebody's daughter is getting pregnant tonight.

Nikolas and I tore that reggae song up. Shit, you would have thought we were on, So You Think You Can Dance, or Dancing With The Stars. We handled our business. I even heard a few people cheering us on. It was times like this I enjoyed being married, but that damn nympho in me won't let me stay faithful.

As we were walking off the dancefloor, I spotted Q standing nearby. He was discreetly serving his street pharmaceuticals in the club. Even though he was blending in well, I knew what was up. The timing couldn't have been perfect.

"*I need those pills.*" I intentionally bumped into him as I walked by.

"My bad." was all I said.

I kept walking with Nikolas towards the bar. When we got to the bar, I told Nikolas I would be right back. I told him I needed to use the restroom.

"You need me to go with you?" he asked with a wide, sexy, smile.

"No baby, I'm straight. I'll be right back."

I kissed Nikolas' sexy lips and shot off towards the bathroom. Q obviously got the hint and met me by the ladies bathroom.

"What's up ma? You looking mad sexy tonight." Q said, licking his light brown lips. He smoked hella weed, which caused his lips to slightly darken; but that nigga was still fine.

"Thanks for the compliment Q. You look sexy yourself in your red Puma tracksuit." I replied seductively.

Q had on a red Puma tracksuit, red and white Puma mid tops, his signature chain with the Q emblem, and his low Caesar fade was sharper than a ballpoint pen. I swear my panties were instantly wet. I don't know what type of connection we have, but it's pretty intense whenever we around each other.

"I saw you out there. You and ole dude was killing that Reggae. I think a part of me got a tad bit jealous." he laughed, fucking with me.

"Whatever nigga." I said, laughing at his silly statement. I shook away my sexual thoughts so I could get straight to business. I ain't trying to get caught talking to Q. That's the last thing I need after the Marco situation at the restaurant.

"Q I need a favor. I don't have much time before Nikolas come looking for me." I said speeding up the conversation.

"Whatever it is, I gotcha ma." he said all sexy, licking his full lips.

"Those lips are so damn sexy. Bitch stay focused."

"Well, I see you working the club tonight and um... Q, I need some of those blue pills." I blurted out. I didn't know how to ask, and I didn't want to say the V word out loud.

I looked over my shoulder to see Nikolas was still at the bar. I was paranoid as fuck. Then I snapped my neck back at Q only to see this nigga dying in laughter. I mean, bent over in fucking tears and shit.

"Q stop fucking laughing. You drawing too much damn attention to us. Pass me the fucking pills now and I will make it worth your while later." I sassed.

"Damn. White boy can't handle your freaky ass. No wonder you be wanting this HARD DICK." He exaggerates the words hard dick because now he knows my husband's dick has a dysfunction.

"Fuckin great!"

"Fuck you Q. He's not white, he's fucking Italian." I snapped at Q. I was now pissed I had said anything at all.

"Same difference ma. Here's five pills. Get ole boy to take one about thirty minutes before time, and he should be able to handle your freaky ass." Q said, passing me a tiny plastic bag with the pills. Then he inconspicuously smacks me on the ass.

"Stop that shit Q. You play too fucking much!" I hissed.

I threw the tiny bag in my purse and walked off. I was so mad, I didn't say thank you. Maybe I was more embarrassed than anything. I guess it was good that I had walked off, because Nikolas ass had come looking for me.

"Hey baby. What took you so long? I was beginning to get worried." he asked with a troubled look.

"Everyone and their mama was in the bathroom Nikolas. The line was long. You know us females are just slow as hell." I said, irritated and trying to calm myself down.

"Aawww!!! Is that why you're looking so pissed off? I knew something was wrong with you. Are you ready to go home beautiful?" Nikolas asked, looking deep into my slanted eyes.

"Yes Nikolas. Let's just go home. I had a wonderful time, but I'm tired baby."

Nikolas simply nodded his head in agreement. He gently

took my small hand in his and we walked out the club. I saw Q out the corner of my eyes as we walked out. I swear that nigga was still laughing while he was serving up another customer.

"He keep fucking with me and he will never get this pussy again. I don't care how good the dick is"

CHAPTER SIX

"THE FOLLOWING MORNING"

Kandy

I was so mad at Q, I forgot all about the damn pills being in my purse. Needless to say I went to bed angry and without sex. It was Sunday morning, so I thought I might as well perform some wifely duties and cook Nikolas breakfast. Nikolas was sound asleep and snoring, so breakfast in bed will be a pleasant surprise.

I walked into my enormous kitchen and placed everything on the kitchen island to start cooking. I decided to cook cheesy grits, French toast, bacon, and scrambled eggs. It wasn't long before I had the kitchen smelling scrumptious. Once everything was done, I placed the food neatly on two bedside trays. Nikolas had a fresh cup of orange juice and I had a fresh cup of coffee.

One thing about me, I had mad cooking skills to be so young; but that's what happens when you're use to feeding yourself. My mother never cooked. I actually taught myself how to cook. Well, I gotta give YouTube some credit along with the cooking channels I love to watch.

As I was getting ready to serve my husband breakfast a bright idea came crossed my mind. I paused with Nikolas breakfast tray, set it down and I tiptoed back inside the bedroom. I peeked inside my purse and glanced at Nikolas. He was still lightly snoring.

"Thank God."

I was very careful not to wake him up. I looked inside my purse, took one blue pill out the tiny bag that Q gave me, then dashed back to the kitchen and started to crush the pill with a shot glass on the countertop. Once the pill was in powder form, I guided it off the countertop into the palm of my hand then placed the powder into Nikolas's orange juice.

"Perfect!!"

I stirred the orange about twenty times to make sure it had blended well. Satisfied my job was completed, I presented Nikolas with breakfast.

"Good morning my love." I beamed.

"I pray the Viagra works. I'm so ready to get fucked."

"Hmmm Mmmm!!! Good morning indeed." Nikolas said, yawning and stretching while noticing the breakfast tray.

I smiled, batting my thick lashes. I stood naked underneath with a tiny, gold robe wrapped around my body. I gently place the tray by Nikolas bedside.

"Breakfast is a thoughtful gesture. Thank you so much my love. The food looks delicious." He said pulling the tray closer and taking a big gulp of orange juice.

"Your welcome bae. Let me go get my tray so I can join you." I said eagerly.

I was beyond ecstatic that he started with the orange juice. The fact he took a large gulp of his juice let me know his dick should be fully erect soon. A bitch was too excited.

"My plan was to take you to Cracker Barrel for breakfast, but I prefer your breakfast any day." Nikolas said, smiling and munching away at the food.

"Aww, you're so sweet. Thanks bae. I'll be right back." I scurried off to the kitchen to get the other food tray.

I returned immediately. I sat on my side of the bed and started eating my breakfast. Every so often I would glance over at Nikolas, and so far he seems to be normal. I wasn't sure how long it would take the drug to take effect, but I was praying it would work soon.

Nikolas had scraped his plate clean, and his glass of orange juice was completely gone. I was still finishing up my breakfast. I wasn't quite done, but I was close. Nikolas got up to take his tray to the kitchen and I still didn't notice a boner.

"That shit ain't working." I was pissed off. I was beginning to wonder what the hell did Q give me.

"I'll be right back Kandy. Everything was delicious. I'm going to take this tray to the kitchen and get some more orange juice. You need anything?" Nikolas asked me.

"Thank you bae. I'm glad you enjoyed your breakfast; and I'm good. I don't need anything." I said, thinking... *"A bitch need some dick, but that ain't going to happen from the looks of it."*

"Okay. I will be right back then." Nikolas said, pecking me on the cheek and exiting the room.

"Damn. Those black Tommy briefs hugging Nikolas' ass riggghht." I thought, checking him out while he was walking out the bedroom. My mind stayed in the fucking gutter. I couldn't help it.

When Nikolas returned to the bedroom my head was down. My face was buried in my phone. I was finishing off my last piece of French toast while scrolling through ratchet Facebook. I was checking out all the drama in our small city, and Facebook told it all.

I saw my bestie Chassidy and that girl Brittney going toe to toe over Ahmad's no good ass. I hate when Chassidy puts her business all over social media. I made a mental note to holla at her later. In my eyes they both were getting played.

I continued to stroll through Facebook. I saw a few other thots arguing with different bitches, bitches going back and forth with their baby daddies, and so on and so on. It was entertaining to say the least. I held my cup of coffee up to my lips, repeatedly taking small sips of my Columbian coffee while laughing at all the drama. Then suddenly I heard Nikolas' baritone voice. He was standing right over me.

"Baby, I'm horny as hell. I don't know what has come over me, but I want you in the worst way Kandy." Nikolas said, standing over me with the biggest dick I've ever seen on him.

My eyes lit up like I was holding the winning ticket to Mega Millions. Nikolas was naked, and his seven inches looked more like ten inches. I almost spit my hot coffee on his ass.

"OH MY FUCKING GAWD! IT WORKED! IT REALLY WORKED!"

"Look at that nice boner. Come here baby, let mommy take care of you." I said, salivating like a dog in heat. I came out of my tiny robe and got on my knees. I was ready. I stay ready. I've been waiting on a moment like this.

I threw my phone down and didn't have a clue where that bitch landed. I no longer gave a damn about social media. It was all about Nicolas and his beautiful, veiny dick. I hungrily took all ten inches into my warm mouth, bobbing up and down.

"Mmhmm." My lips, jaw muscles, tongue and suction was the truth. I was sucking that dick good.

That shit was poking down my throat and tickling my tonsils, but I enjoyed every moment. Nikolas' confidence was on one hundred because he fucked my face like he forgot it was attached to my neck.

"I can get use to this." I thought, humming on Nikolas' dick.

I love that aggressive shit. Then suddenly Nikolas made an unexpected move. He removed my full lips off his engorged dick, snatched me up by my curly hair tresses and tossed my naked body over his wide shoulders. He walked me to the bed then threw me roughly unto the mattress.

Nikolas pinned my legs far behind my head and fucked me like I never been fucked before. I mean I've had BIGGER, but not BETTER. Viagra put Nikolas on the fucking map. He always bickering he didn't need no damn Viagra, but the hell he says. To keep me happy, he better get used to it.

We ended up fucking for hours. Nikolas put me in every position possible, and he had worked my little ass like I was his personal sex toy. For the first time of our marriage, I had multiple orgasms. In my head I was chanting, *"Go Nikolas. Go Nikolas."*

I was so tired of fucking. I tapped out. My pussy was swoll and my shit was sore. He put a hurting on my ass, but in a good way. I didn't know his old ass had it in him. We had anal sex, oral sex, sixty-eight, sixty-nine, doggy style, reversed cowgirl, missionary style, standing up, sitting down, in the shower, on the floor, and the list goes on. You name it, we did it.

That Viagra gave our sex life fireworks! I've started something, because that was just the beginning. I know my husband thinks he got his mojo back, but nah; he had some assistance. Now I gotta figured out how I'm going to tell Nicolas I slipped him some V.

"I think I'll wait till I'm out of pills. Hell, I still have four more

to go." I thought with a devious smile.

CHAPTER SEVEN

"WHO'S THE NYMPHO NOW?"

Kandy

I can't believe Friday has rolled back around. This week went by like a flash, and I'm officially out of Viagra. I gave Nikolas his last pill in a smoothie last night. I guess that shit was still in his system, because this morning he got some pussy to go and it was off the chain. Shit, I think he's the damn nympho now!

Nikolas been bragging, all week how great our sex has been. Poor dude still thinks his mojo has returned. I must admit, I have REALLY enjoyed Nikolas' sex. If I had known then what I know now, I would have been gotten Nikolas some V.

Nikolas been tearing my shit up twice every single day. I had to purchase some perineal cooling pads so my pussy and anal could recover when weren't fucking. Hell, my coochie so sore I've been faithful all week. My entire week consisted of hardcore fucking, perineal cooling pads, and Epsom salt baths.

Chassidy been hitting me up like crazy. I haven't had time to call her back. I think she wants a round two, but I'm good. I gotta let her know our lesbo moment was a onetime thing.

"She needs to get over it."

The last thing I want to do is to fuck up my friendship with Chassidy. She already said she was in love with me, so there's no need to complicate things further with sex. I plan on calling her soon... after I get some breakfast. It's early and that heifer probably still sleep. Chassidy ain't never been a morning person.

I ended up having to block Marco's crazy ass. He started to send threatening messages. That nigga act like his world coming to an end over some anal. I swear I regret fucking with him. He's acting like a bitch about the situation. It is what it is, and that's it.

Q keeps calling and texting, but I've been boxing him and ignoring his kinky messages. I'm still in my feelings about last week at the club, but I need to get at him soon because I need some more Viagra.

As much as I hate to admit it, I need Q. I guess I gotta swallow my pride, because I need a full re-up of V. Hell, I need a full thirty day supply of Viagra since I see that shit actually works.

I reluctantly got up outta bed. I was still partially nude. The only thing I was wearing was Nicolas' oversized T-shirt. I love sleeping in Nikolas' cologne filled T-shirts. I looked in the mirror at my disheveled hair and fingered my loose, shoulder length locks.

Even though my natural curls were beautiful, I hated them. I mean, I get nice compliments about my hair, but I get so tired of looking like the black Shirley Temple. All these curls make me look hella young, and that's a downfall when you're married to an older man. I get so annoyed at the sly remarks. Sometimes people comments are racist. Then there's folks mistaking me for

Nikolas's adopted daughter.

"So annoying and rude."

It's not cute for a wife to get mistaken as the husband's daughter. What a joke. The shit is nerve wrecking. How can people miss my fat ass wedding ring? Unless they're being funny! I made a mental note to holla at my mom. I need to change up my hair ASAP. Maybe she can give me a short, sexy look. I'm thinking Keri Hilson, Halle Berry, Keyshia Cole, Jada Pickett type of hairdo. It's time I rocked a more mature look.

My stomach started to growl, reminding me it was time for breakfast. I slipped out of the cologne filled T-shirt and hopped in the shower. After ten minutes, I stepped out the shower, wrapped myself in a towel and I used a wide tooth comb to go through my damp hair. I decided for now to wear my hair down in loose curls, with a side part.

Now that my hair is out the way, I walked over to my closet. I grabbed my white low rider jeans, a white Bebe crop top, and my white and gold Bebe sandals. I sprayed a few squirts of Bebe Wish & Dreams perfume on then left the house, heading to Hardees for some breakfast. It literally felt like I was starving, but that's a norm for me.

"I'm greedy as hell to be so little."

On my way to Hardee's my phone started to ring *"Fuckkk... its Chassidy calling AGAIN! She never calls this damn early. I thought that bitch was sleep. Is it that serious? It's ten in the morning."* I thought as I answered.

"What's up bestie?" I answered, sucking my teeth. I had Chassidy on my car's Bluetooth while dipping through the light morning traffic.

"Damn bitch! Trying to get in touch with you is harder than getting VIP tickets for Beyoncé and Jay-Z's world tour. I been trying to holla at your lil ass all week." Chassidy complained.

"My bad Chassidy. I been meaning to call you. What happened between us was a onetime thing. I can't be fucking up our friendship with sex." I said, pulling into Hardee's parking lot.

"Bitch, you arrogant as hell. This ain't got shit to do with me fucking you. Is that why you've been ignoring my calls? I mean, yeah I love you, and your pussy is fiyah; but I ain't tripping on that shit." she said, clearly hurt. Now I'm more confused.

"Then what is the urgency of this phone call?"

"Okay. First of all, I haven't been ignoring your calls. I just had a lot going on at home Chassidy. I'm sorry about the assumption. Just hold on, let me pull over so we can talk. I'm in Hardee's parking lot. I was getting ready to order breakfast, but it can wait." I said apprehensively. I parked my vehicle, so I could hear her out.

"I just parked Chassidy. Now tell me what's going on." I demanded. I heard her let out a deep sigh before she spoke.

"I don't know when it happened, but that fuck nigga is out of prison. I knew you couldn't have had an inkling because you ain't said shit. I been blowing up your phone bestie 'cause you know how small Gadsden is. It's only a matter of time before you run into his ass."

"Chassidy, who hell are you talking about? Hell, it's a lot of niggas in and out of prison. You ranting on and on, but not once have you said a damn name. Who the fuck are you talking about?"

"Bitch, will you please stop acting slow. I'm talking about the nigga who took your damn virginity by force. The same nigga that killed your father. Wayne is out of prison bitch, and you know his pedophile ass is going to be looking for you."

I literally felt the life drain from my entire body. I queasily slumped down in the seat of my car. Suddenly I felt like the same defenseless, eleven-year-old that was raped by her father's best friend. I was visibly shaken up, and I had every right to be.

Ten years ago Wayne took my virginity. I was only eleven years. Wayne first started fondling me when I was ten years old. I guess he was grooming me so he could take advantage of me later. It started off with him kissing me, licking my pussy, and then fingering me. When that wasn't good enough, that nigga raped me.

The only two people I told about Wayne is my father and my bestie Chassidy. The day I confessed my secret to my father, he went crazy. He couldn't believe a nigga he considered his brother would commit such a heinous act. He promised that nigga would pay for hurting me.

He went straight to Wayne's house. They got into a heated fight, guns were drawn, and my father was murdered. Wayne shot him directly in his heart at point blank range. My father never got a chance to tell my mom about the rape before he was murdered by Wayne.

We loss everything after my father was murdered. We went from living large to housing projects. I never told my mom the real reason behind my father's murder. I kept that ugly secret out of shame and guilt. Everyone presumed since my father and Wayne were big street hustlas and partnas that they had a disagreement about the business and one thing led to another.

"I'm paranoid as fuck right now and my day is ruined." I was sitting in my car zoned out.

"Kandy! Kandy! Kandy!" Chassidy screamed, getting louder each time she called my name.

"WHAT?!?!?" I screamed out with hot tears streaming down my face.

"WE GONNA MAKE THAT NIGGA WAYNE PAY. THAT'S WHAT!" she shot back with malice.

"You damn right bestie. Wayne took my innocence, my father; and I will be DAMNED if he takes my sanity. That nigga gots to go. Revenge will be served cold as ice, and that nigga will never see it coming." I said in a malicious tone.

"Fuck breakfast!!!"

My appetite was instantly gone. I peeled out of Hardee's parking lot and headed home to get my thoughts together.

"On my daddy, that nigga gots to die."

After hanging up with Chassidy, I immediately called my mother and filled her in about Wayne getting release from prison. My mother was worried. She knows how close my father was to me, and she's afraid I will retaliate. She has no clue about the molestation and rape, but I will handle Wayne my damn self. I'm talking street justice. Even though I've never owned a gun a day in life, that shit is about to change ASAP!!!

CHAPTER EIGHT

"A DANGEROUS OBSESSION"

Marco

I'm so fucked up in the head. I keep calling Kandy, but she won't answer. It's driving me crazy. I know she see; I've been calling her ass.

"I'm probably blocked knowing Kandy."

Ever since she's been ignoring my calls, I've been stalking her ass. I've been following Kandy for weeks. She has become my everyday obsession. In these past weeks, I've learned a lot about the busy Kandy Kane. That young hoe fucking more than me and the dentist.

I mean, I knew Kandy's hoe ass was married when we first started to fuck. It didn't matter. We were only supposed to have paid, casual sex; but I need her on my team permanently. I ain't never had a bitch to drop me the way Kandy dropped me. Then she bopping all over town. That shit is foul and fuck, and my ego is bruised.

I understand Kandy was mad when my girl got her number out my phone, but I checked Tyesha snooping ass for calling Kandy. I told her if she EVER go through my phone again and call ANYONE, I'll choke that pretty ass to sleep.

That bitch know I ain't playing with her short ass either. She useless as a girlfriend, but she's sexy as hell. I only keep her around to kill the downlow rumors that's been spreading like wildfire about me. These young niggas round here talk too damn much, but I'll never admit to SHIT!

I'm that nigga that chicks love to chase. I'm thirty years old, 6'2 in height, light complected, curly hair, with green slanted eyes. I love women, but I have a secret fetish. I have an anal fascination. My girl Tyesha ain't down with me fucking her in the ass. She said my dick too big, so I'm constantly cheating.

You know my bitch had the nerve to ask me if I was gay. Man, I slapped her ass so hard she lost her front tooth. Don't worry, I got that shit crowned. She can't be my girl looking like a fucking crackhead.

One thing about Kandy... she doesn't question me, nor has she ever judged me; and I kept her pockets laced. Kandy can take anal like a 'G', and I miss it. I miss her! Shid, from time to time I do fuck young niggas in the ass. SO FUCKING WHAT! That doesn't make me gay. As long as I'm not taking dick, I'm not gay... POINT, BLANK, PERIOD!

I had stopped fucking with men when Kandy came into the picture; but I've recently started back after she cut me loose. When it comes to anal, gender never mattered to me. Pussy doesn't grip my dick the way ass do. It's a guaranteed orgasm every time I get some sweet ass. Let me reiterate. No I'm not GAY!

Can you believe I ain't never had Kandy's young pussy? I wouldn't mind trying it out since she's passing it around like a blunt. If I can get Kandy back, I promised myself I'll leave Tyesha and these young niggas alone for good. Kandy's ass was tighter than Virgin Mary. Besides, fucking men be making me feel guilty and shit. I don't like titles and categories when it comes to my sexuality. Let me be me.

Damn this world is so fucking judgmental. I do know one thing, it's time to stop stalking Kandy. That shit ain't getting me nowhere. I need a one on one with her, and I plan on getting at her... REAL SOON!

"Damn I miss my Kandy Kane."

CHAPTER NINE

"WILDING OUT"

Kandy

E ver since Chassidy told me about Wayne getting released from prison, a bitch been paranoid. I've been stressed out. Most bitches go on a shopping spree. Hell, I been on a fucking spree. I've been losing my mind. I even purchased a gun in case I ran into Wayne's sorry ass. I plan to shoot first and ask questions later.

Even though the details are fuzzy from ten years ago. They keep replaying in my head. I've been wrecking my brain on how to make that fuck nigga pay for killing my father, raping and molesting me. Wayne must be laying low, 'cause as small as this town is, I haven't seen him once.

My addickion is worse than ever. I even did a few one night stands with random niggas. It's like I don't give a fuck anymore, and I'm being careless with the shit. I'm surprised Nikolas hasn't heard shit bout me. The streets talk, and people round here snitch about every thang.

I put my bruised feelings to the side and I hollered at Q.

He gave me a nice re-up of Viagra, and we've been fucking every other day since then. I even fucked Chassidy again after saying I wouldn't, and I've managed to fuck Nikolas every single day.

I've been wilding out! My pussy been taking a straight beat down. It's the same way my heart feels. I been numbing the pain of my past with alcohol, popping Xanax bars, and of course lots of sex. I know it's ironic that I turned to sex, being a victim of sexual abuse; but that's my coping mechanism. Sex is a temporary fix, but my pain seems permanent.

I finally confessed to Nikolas about secretly giving him crushed Viagra. Hell, I didn't have much choice. He knew something was wrong when he had a five hour erection. I fucked up and gave Nikolas twice the dosage accidently. My reckless mistake ended up sending him to Gadsden Regional Emergency Room. It looked like an episode of, "Sex Sent Me To The ER."

Nikolas had a hard on that wouldn't go down no matter how long we fucked. Then he started to have a massive headache, his dick was hurting, and his vision was getting blurry. It was almost like he was going blind. I was scared as hell.

To make a long story short, the doctor stuck a long ass needle in his dick to relieve the built up pressure. That shit looked painful, and I had to look away. His ass was screaming like a bitch in labor and delivery. By the time it was all over Nikolas was furious at me, but most of all he felt humiliated. This town small so people talk. I really felt bad, but it was already done. There's was nothing I could do or say except I was sorry.

By the time we got home, which was the following day, we had the BIGGEST argument. He gave me the he felt betrayed speech; the incident could hurt his dental practice, yada yada. Hell, I felt betrayed too in the fucking bedroom; and if he found out about my booty buddies, betrayal will have a whole new meaning.

Since Nikolas got released from the hospital, we haven't been on speaking terms. Not for real; a hey here, and a bye there, is about it. Then you already know his dick is out of commission at least for a couple days or more. Then I'm sure when we do have sex, we will be back to having BORING SEX.

I know I might have been wrong or whatever, but I was trying to help the erectile dysfunction that Nikolas won't admit to having. If he had fixed the problem, I wouldn't have tried to fix it myself. Then he can't lie, we were having the best sex ever. Well, until I accidently overdosed him on V.

CHAPTER TEN

"CAN'T CATCH A BREAK"

Kandy

This morning was the same as others. Nikolas went to work with the same dry ass goodbye. This shit been going on now for almost two weeks since his incident. My good life as I know it, might be coming to an end.

Nikolas ain't never been so livid with me. He hasn't asked for sex, and he hasn't kissed me or touched me in any affectionate way. I can't read him. The sad thing is, I was just getting used to this lavish life. My nice home of 4000 square feet, my car, designer clothes and shoes could all be gone in a blink of an eye.

Nikolas confirmed what I already assumed, and that was his coworkers, family and friends heard about the Viagra and his overnight stay in the hospital. I'm not sure if he will ever forgive me. I feel like my marriage is broken.

"Damn! One step forward and five steps backwards. I can't catch a break for shit! I wouldn't be surprised if he filed for divorce over this shit!"

I glanced at my phone and saw it was almost noon. Shit, I

was supposed to be having lunch with Chassidy at Logan's Road-house, but I need to talk to my mother. I shot Chassidy a text, telling her I will have to take a raincheck on lunch and I had something important I needed to handle.

I need to get my ass up, and head straight to my mothers. I have to tell her exactly what my father couldn't tell her before he was murdered. I need to confess to my mother what's been eating me up for the past ten years.

"On everything I love, this secret is coming out TODAY."

I brushed my teeth, washed my face and threw on a blue jean romper. Looking at my galore shoe shelf, I picked out my peanut butter Gladiator sandals. Then I pulled my hair up in a high, curly ponytail.

"I still gotta get my mother to cut this shit." I thought, fluffing out my girlish ponytail.

Grabbing my purse, I made sure my hot pink 9mm was tucked inside. Then I tossed my phone in my purse and grabbed my key fob. Now I was ready to head to mothers, or so I thought.

As soon as I opened my door, psycho Marco was standing in my doorway. I haven't heard from him since I blocked him. I really thought he got the message. OBVIOUSLY NOT!! I can't believe he had the audacity to show up at my house. Then this crazy muthafucka looking like he hasn't eaten or slept in weeks.

"This nigga on some creep shit. I wonder how long he's been standing outside my door."

"Marco, what the fuck are you doing here?" I questioned with my face scrunched up. I slid my right hand inside my purse. If I had to bust a cap in this idiot, I would. I ain't got time for this shit,

I'm trying to get to my mother's house.

"I had to come see you. Baby you left me no choice. I've been reaching out to you, but you blocked a nigga. I want to talk to you in person about how things went down. I need to clear the air and make this shit right between us. I miss you Kandy." he said, stammering all over his words.

He's such a fucking pussy. Nigga standing on my front porch, in front of all my white nosey neighbors, like my black ass ain't married. I'm already two seconds away from a divorce. I don't need this shit. I gotta get Marco away from my damn house by any means necessary; even if that means lying to his pathetic face.

"Sometimes you gotta play the fool to fool the fool."

"Look Marco, you clearly forgot I'm married. You can't be showing up on my door step, expecting me to talk to you. Then we all out in the open and shit. I tell you what, I'll setup a time when we can talk if you promise not to ever come back to my house. I will even take your number off the block list if you leave, NOW!" I said, taking my hand off my gun and pulling my phone out of my purse.

"You mean that shit Kandy?" he asked skeptically.

"Yes, look! I'm taking you off the blocked list right now." I said going through my block list and removing his name so he could see me doing it.

"Okay, it's a deal Kandy. Don't have me waiting too long to hear from you. I'm serious, we gotta talk." he said with a quarter of a smile. He had a look of liberation written across his handsome face. I'm just glad he fell for the lie I fed him.

"Why the fine niggas always crazy as fuck?" I asked myself.

"I won't have you waiting long Marco. Talk to you soon." I said, waving him off with the most genuine smile I could muster up. I made sure to watch him leave before I got into my car. I couldn't have psycho Marco following me.

"Today is his lucky day. For a moment I thought I was going to have to pop his yellow ass on my front porch."

After I made sure I didn't see Marco blue mustang anywhere in sight, I locked my front door. Then I shot my mother a text letting her know I was coming over and it was important. Once she responded okay, I got in my car heading to the west side.

CHAPTER ELEVEN

"BOTTLED UP PAIN"

Kandy

I pulled up to my mother's housing project. Summer time had everyone hanging out. Kids were playing, dudes were drinking, smoking, shooting dice on the sidewalk, and hoochie mamas were walking around with their booty shorts and baby strollers. It's was a typical day in the hood.

A few niggas yelled my name. I simply gave a head nod as I continued walking towards my mother's door. I had a key, so there was no need for me to knock. I simply pulled my key out my purse and unlocked the door to my mother's project.

"Hey mom." I said, noticing she was doing hair.

"Hey Kandy. You look cute. I'm almost done with Tyesha's hair. Give me about five minutes."

"Okay." I responded, taking a seat on the black leather sofa. My mother might have stayed in the projects, but she had that shit decked out like a high-end apartment. She's a neat freak, so her place stays spotless.

My mother was finishing up her last faux loc on some random chick's hair. I've never seen the bitch a day in my life; but as soon my mother said my name, her head snapped in my direction. Her face turned beet red, like we had some sort of beef.

"Um what the fuck is this red heifer problem?" I pondered.

The chick clearly couldn't stand the sight of me for whatever reason. She mean mugged me and rolled her eyes; but remained in the chair, fuming in silence. It was as if she couldn't wait till my mother finished her hair. I kept my eyes trained on her, because if she steps to me wrong she's gonna regret that shit.

As soon as my mother finished up the last faux loc, she collected her money from the Tyesha chick. Then the drama began. The very moment my mother pocketed the money was the instant this bitch stood up on some Laila Ali shit. She started walking her short, red ass in my direction, so I stood the fuck up. I was ready for whatever.

"So, you the infamous slut Kandy. I can't stand your hoe ass. You been fucking my man. You the bitch causing me and my man problems. I plan to handle your lanky looking ass." she spat, rubbing her small bulge.

I assume the heifer is pregnant; but what I don't have time for is playing games with her. Pregnant or not, she can get popped the way I feel right now.

"Oh, hell nah lil bitch. If you got beef with my daughter you got beef with me. You ain't...," my mother tried to say, but I cut her off immediately.

"Unh, Unh... I got this mama! Let me handle this little bitch." I said, sliding my hand in my purse. I step close enough, so Tyesha could taste the words as I spit them out.

"Bitch I don't know your short ass, but it's clear you know

me. You picked the right fucking day to step to me, because I'm in the mood to hurt somebody. I don't give a damn about your so call man; ESPECIALLY if his name ain't Nikolas. Do yourself a favor and get the fuck out my mother's apartment before you get yourself popped!" I screamed, directing my gun at her head.

"Stay away from Marco hoe. Can't you see I'm pregnant with his baby." she screamed with tears running down her reddened face. Tyesha is a beautiful chick, but that bitch is naïve as fuck.

"Ain't no way in hell I will give that gay nigga a baby." I silently spat.

"You talking about the same nigga that's stalking me? Nigga was just on my doorstep begging. You funny as fuck. Bitch, tell that nigga to stay away from me. Check ya nigga bitch. He's the one begging to be with me. I give two fucks about his gay ass."

"JUST LEAVE US THE FUCK ALONE!" she yelled, crying like a baby. Then her scary ass sprinted out my mother's front door.

I laughed at her dramatic ass, then placed my gun back in my purse. I wasn't going to shoot her, but it was best she didn't push me. I have a lot of built up anger in me, and I didn't need to be sent over the edge.

"Sorry about the drama mom." I normally don't curse in front of my mother, and if I do it's a slip up.

"Hell, don't worry about that shit Kandy. Tyesha betta not bring her red ass back over here. I ain't got time for her silly girl drama. Niggas gonna be niggas. The sooner she realizes that, the better she'll be." my mother said, taking a seat. "So, what's up baby girl? What you wanna talk about?" she questioned, firing up a Newport cigarette.

I sat down beside my mother and tried to prepare her the best I could about the rape and molestation.

"Mom, what I'm about to tell you is going to change everything you thought you knew regarding the death of my father. I've held onto this pain for over ten years. It's time you know the truth." I said getting choked up.

My mother pulled the ash tray, on the coffee table, close to her, and proceed to put out her lit cigarette. She blew the last of her smoke directly into the air.

"Kandy what exactly are you trying to tell me? What happened to Lorenzo is not your fault." my mother said, calling my father by his real name.

She studied my face as hot tears streamed, burning my eye sockets like fire. "Kandy baby, what's the matter? Tell me!!!" she screamed out in panic.

My mother had no idea what was going on. She just grabbed my small frame and put me in her loving arms. I was sobbing out loud while reliving a nightmare.

"It's okay baby, let it out. Whatever it is, let it out Kandy. We can deal with it!" she said rocking me like a baby.

I began wiping the tears from my wet face. I needed to be strong. I had to get the truth out no matter how painful it was.

I asked God to give me the courage. It was crucial that I told my mother about my childhood abuse; so I swallowed the large lump the set in my throat and took a deep breath before I decided to make my confession.

"Mom, I'm a victim of sexual abuse."

"DID WHAT???!" she screamed out in shock.

"It's true mama. I remember when I was first molested. I was only ten years old. I couldn't comprehend why a grown ass man would touch me the way he did. The molestation turned into rape when I was eleven. He took my innocence mama. I was only a child. It was supposed to be our little secret; until I told my father EVERYTHING."

"Oh my Godddddddd baby! Oh my Godddddddd!" my mother screams at the top of her lungs. She runs all over the place screaming to God. "Why my baby God?" She stretched her arms up as if she was questioning God.

"I never wanted to tell you mama. I'm so broken inside. Being exposed to sex at such a young age turned me into a hoe mama. I have a weird addiction to sex, and I feel like I'm damaged goods mama. I HATE THE PERSON I AM, AND HE'S THE FUCKING BLAME!" I continue to cry out, shaking in agonizing pain. I still hadn't said his name.

My mother grabbed me by the shoulders forcing me to look her directly in her eyes. Snot and tears were everywhere. My secret has devastated my mother.

"It's not your fault baby. Who did this to you Kandy? Who the fuck messed with my baby girl?!" she screamed out, then starts holding her chest. It was like her heart could explode.

I stared into mama's big brown, swollen eyes. "My father died trying to get revenge for me. It was Wayne mama. Wayne molested and raped me." I sobbed even louder, but my mother started mumbling to herself.

"No, No, No! Not Wayne!!! Why would he hurt you? Why would he hurt his flesh and blood?" she looked shocked and confused.

"Could she be in denial?"

"Mama how the hell is daddy's ex-bestfriend my flesh and blood; and why are you looking like you don't believe me? That nigga raped me and killed my father mama. He's going to pay for what he did to me, and he's going to pay for killing my father!" I screamed, taken back at her reaction.

Suddenly there was a loud knock at mama's door. I was having a whole melt down, and my mama looked like she had lost part of mind.

"I believe you Kandy, but something is not adding up. If what you say is true, I will kill Wayne my damn self" she said with venom dripping off her fuming tongue.

"Let me see who's at the door."

Mother reluctantly answered the door. She had the meanest scowl I've ever seen. As soon as she opened the door, there stood the nigga that took everything from me. It was Wayne in the flesh!

CHAPTER TWELVE

"THE TRUTH IS EXPOSED"

Kandy

"**Y**our muthafucking ears must have been burning. Come on in Wayne. Ion know whatcha doing here but we have MUCH to discuss nigga." my mother hissed, stepping to the side so Wayne could enter.

Her tears had dried up, and now all I could see is pure rage. Unlike my mother, she was thick as hell. She worked out faithfully at Planet Fitness. She reminded me of the actress Angela Bassett. Everyone in Gadsden knew about Gina O'Neil. Back in the days she could take down a nigga with her bare hands, but she could finesse that same nigga with her beauty. My mother wasn't no joke, and I can imagine she was still fye with her paws.

I stared that nigga Wayne down. He walked in looking like a replica of the rapper Warren G. He was fresh in designer clothes, considering he ain't been out of prison long. His head was shaved bald. He had a thin beard and a goatee.

I can't believe this nigga hurt me. He was like an uncle to me. If I had infrared eyes, I would have burnt a hole straight into his soul. I hated him with every breath within me. He walked in, looking at me with the deepest sympathy in his hazel eyes. I don't know what was up with that, but he can save his fucking sympathy.

He walked inside as my mother slammed the door shut with so much force that every picture on the wall shuddered. Hell, she scared me. I knew the odds of Wayne walking out of here were slim to fucking none! He's gonna get exactly what the fuck he deserves... DEATH!

It seems like time my mother shut the door she went the fuck off. "You no good piece of shit. Kandy just told me the fucking truth! How could you hurt Kandy? You out of all people should have been protecting her. You raped and molested my daughter! You sick piece of shit!" she screams, and whaps Wayne across the face so hard I swear to God I could see her hand print.

"Gina, what the hell are you talking about? I could never hurt Kandy. Kandy, what did you tell your mother?" he asked with teary, concerned and confused eyes.

"This nigga looks mighty convincing, playing dumb and shit." I thought, getting angrier by the second.

"What the hell you mean? I told my mother the fucking truth. I told her you killed my father because I told him about you molesting and raping me. He died trying to protect me from a monster. I fucking hate you. You're an apex predator. A low life pedophile, and you won't breathe another day to hurt another child or kill another person." I said with my nostrils flaring in and out.

I quickly slid my hand in my purse and pulled out my gun. I pointed the pink 9mm straight at that nigga. I been waiting ten years for this day. The day to avenge my father's death, and to rock my rapist to sleep for an eternity.

"Hold up!!! Wait, wait, wait Kandy. Look at me!" he demanded, pointing towards his chest. "If I did the things you said I did, I muthafucking deserve to die; but I need you to REMEMBER baby girl. Think back to the day it all happened."

"What the fuck he mean... think back?"

Wayne looked over at my mother. "Gina, I promise you I would never hurt her a hair on her body, and you should know that for a fact." Wayne looks back at me. "Kandy, you must have suppressed your memories because the truth hurts too bad for you to remember."

"Suppressed my memories my ass. I know what the fuck happened! I was there!" I snapped.

"Kandy, I was there too; and I remember everything like it was yesterday. I lived with the horrific memory every day I spent in prison. I killed Lorenzo to protect you! Think back Kandy!" He roared, ignoring the gun I had pointed towards him.

"Mom, he's lying! He's fucking lying!" I yelled. The gun was trembling in my small hands. My eyes darted back and forth. I just wanted to kill him.

"Gina hunni, I tried to tell you over and over again for the entire ten years I've been locked up; but you would never accept my calls. I came over here so I could tell you the truth in person. It's good you're here Kandy. You both need to hear the real reason why I killed Lorenzo punk ass." he said, getting choked up, as he spoke to me and my mother.

"Kandy, all I need for you and your mother to do is to hear me out. That's all!!! Then you can decide from there what my fate is." Wayne said with a look of defeat.

"Lower your gun Kandy. Let's hear his ass out; and if what he says doesn't add up, I'll personally put the same hole through his heart as he did Lorenzo's." she spoke coldly.

Against my will, I decided to lower my gun. Wayne exhaled

deeply. We all stood in the living room. Everyone's emotions were at an all-time high. We listened intently as Wayne began telling his version of what happened ten years ago.

Ten years ago

"Lorenzo and I were big time bosses. We pushed dope harder than anyone in the southeast of the U.S. We were partnas, and we spreading our territory like crazy. We were brothers; not by blood, but by loyalty. Kandy, you have always been the apple of Lorenzo's eye. I'm almost certain he overheard your mother Gina, and I talking one day over the phone. I saw a change in him, and I suppose that was the first time he touched you." he said sadly.

"Mom, what is Wayne talking about?" I hissed, but she remained silent. She started to look uneasy. Ignoring my question, she spoke out to Wayne.

"Keep going Wayne. Get to the day of the shooting." she said, narrowing her eyes at Wayne.

"Alright, we can come back to that conversation. On the day of the shooting Gina, you were at home and Kandy was with Lorenzo. That wasn't strange, because he always had Kandy with him; even at the trap houses. I didn't approve of the shit, but it was what it was at the time. We had just bought a new trap house for the Northside. Everything was good to go; we just needed to set up the surveillance, assign a Lieutenant and get some soldiers to run that bitch. He asked me to set the meeting up to get everything in order for the new trap. I was like bet. I left the trap. At the time, Lorenzo was busy setting up the surveillance cameras. My plan was to put the perfect team together and setup a meeting, but that was after I hit up Popeye's. Kandy, when I left the trap you was sitting Indian style on the floor in a yellow sundress playing with your iPad. I think I was gone about thirty minutes before I realized I left my phone. I was like fuck it, I was already at Popeye's. I decided to go ahead and eat; then go back, grab my phone, once I finished eating my three piece snack." Wayne paused for a moment.

His eyes were filled with so much agony. It was like he could barely muster up the words to finish.

"Then what happened Wayne?" my mother questioned, with a raised brow. Her upper lip was curled up in disdain.

My mind started to rewind to the year 2008. Memories I never knew were there started to resurface. I remembered playing Candy Crush on my iPad in the trap house. I remember sitting in the middle of the floor in my yellow sundress.

I recall my father being angry and yelling at me after Wayne left. Crocodile tears were flowing. I grabbed my mouth to prevent a scream. That day was becoming clearer. I was on a verge of a mental breakdown, but I continued to listen.

"After I ate, I went back to the trap to retrieve my phone. As soon as I exited my car, Gina all I could hear were high pitched, bone chilling screams." Wayne's jaw began to twitch, and his eyes turned blood shot red. "I recognized the screams instantly. The screams sounded young and childlike. They were Kandy's screams Gina. I jumped out my burgundy Lexus and ran like hell inside the trap house. What I saw hurt me so bad, all I could see was red. It had to be a bloody fucking murder. I couldn't let that nigga live Gina." he said with hot tears streaming down his angry face.

"WHAT DID YOU SEE?" my mom asked frantically.

"Gina...Lorenzo was between Kandy's legs, humping away while she screamed immensely. I went CRRRAAAZZY. I snatched that punk ass bitch off Kandy and threw his hoe ass like a rag to the floor. I beat that nigga's ass so bad he probably would have died from internal injuries even if I hadn't shot him in the heart. I witnessed him raping Kandy, and when I grabbed my gun to shoot him, Kandy asked me for my gun and I gave it to her. She shot that nigga straight in his dick and she said..."

"Stop, stop stop!!! Oh my God! All these years I've blamed you Wayne. For ten years I blamed you!" I cried out after realizing what really happened. "Mom, I remember every fucking thing. I remember clear as day. Wayne, I know exactly what I said after I shot him. I looked down at the piece of shit and screamed at the top of my lungs. I HATE YOU LORENZO AND YOU'VE HURT ME FOR THE LAST TIME! That's when you took the smoking gun from me and shot Lorenzo a second time, point blank range directly in the heart." I said choking on the words that spewed from my mouth. Wayne nodded in agreement.

"I swear foe God that's exactly what happened." Wayne said with a broken heart. I can imagine it hurt him to retell the story. Mom started to breakdown bad. It pained me to see her tore up like that.

"Lorenzo hurt my baby. Lord Jesus that nigga touched my baby." my mother sobbed out loud.

This was the most emotional moment I've had since my father raped me. After my father was killed, Wayne is the one who took care of me. My mind had made Wayne the villain, but he's a fucking hero.

"Mom, my father hurt me sooooo bad." I said whimpering. "I remember washing my hands and fingernails with peroxide and a toothbrush, then I showered like three times. My old clothes were burned, and a booster brought me new clothes to the trap. After I was completely dressed, Wayne you called your sister Tonia. She took me home after all the evidence of my rape was destroyed. Then I suppose my young mind had a breakdown, recreating a story only my mind could handle. I'm so sorry Wayne."

"No apologies necessary baby girl. I apologize I wasn't there sooner. Death was too good for that nigga. I really should have tortured his ass first."

"And I wish I was the one who put the bullet through my

father's evil heart." I snapped.

"I never got a chance to explain what happened. In the midst of my sister taking you home, the police were called by a neighbor I guess. I was questioned, and to protect you Kandy, I never mentioned why I killed Lorenzo. I just told the police he deserved worse than death. I took a ten year plea deal. I served my ten years with no remorse, and I would do it all again to protect you Kandy."

"That bastard! That heartless bastard! Rot in fucking hell Lorenzo! Rot in fucking hell!" My mother screamed hysterically.

My mind had overflowed with horrible memories. I've accepted the truth. My father was a real life boogey man. He was a Drug Lord by day, and a pedophile by night. Wayne did me a favor the day he sent his soul to hell.

"Wayne, mom; I'm so sorry for not telling you the truth sooner. I should have told you the first time he touched me." I cried out in pain.

"No baby, don't blame yourself. I should have paid more attention to Lorenzo. He had gotten real possessive over you. I feel I'm the one to blame." my mother said all choked up.

We all went and set down on the sofa. I set in the middle. My mother softly stroked my hair, consoling me the best she could.

Wayne was mumbling, "This could have been prevented." I didn't understand what he meant but I would soon find out.

"I remember being so scared to tell you mother, because he said he would kill us both. I remember the day he savagely raped me. The unbearable pain as he roughly entered my young vagina. He kept yelling I was a slut like my mother and that he wasn't my real father." I cried out to my mom and Wayne.

"Oh my God! He knew Wayne! He fucking knew! That's why he hurt Kandy!" my mother screams out to Wayne.

"What the fuck are they hiding from me?"

"I need to know the truth Wayne and mom. What you mean he knew mother; and what you mean it could have been prevented Wayne? What are you two not telling me? If Lorenzo O'Neil ain't my biological father... who the fuck is my father?" I asked angrily.

My mother looked at Wayne and Wayne looked back at my mother. They gave each other a knowing look.

"Tell me the fucking truth; NOW!" I went off on the both of them.

Wayne looked at me and said, "Kandy... Lorenzo must have figured it out. The phone conversation he heard was your mother telling me I was your father and not Lorenzo. She found out Lorenzo was sterile after they kept trying for a second child. I... AM... YOUR... FATHER!!!!" His words cut like a razor and stung like a bee. My mother place her hands over her face in shame.

"Are you two fucking kidding me right now?" I spat.

"Baby, please let us explain." My mother broke down crying. I could see the regret written on both of their faces, but they couldn't begin to see or feel the pain of their betrayal!!!

If the timing couldn't have been any worst, my phone started to chime. I glanced at the screen and it was Nikolas. I was trying to decide if I should answer it or not. I already had so much going on. Against my better judgement I answered the phone.

"Everyone just chill out. I gotta take this call. It's my fucking husband!" I yelled over them trying to explain.

"Hi baby." I said trying to sound normal as possible.

"Save it Kandy. Don't worry about coming home EVER! I will have your shit shipped to those filthy projects you grew up in. You think I wouldn't find out the truth about that nigga Marco! Tyesha came to my office and told me the truth. You had it all, but you had to be greedy! What's the saying all the rappers say?

Hmmm like me think. You can't turn a hoe into a housewife. I'm filing for an annulment immediately. You won't get one cent of my fucking money!!!" he yelled and hangs up the phone.

In total shocked I looked at the phone. I realized Nikolas was no longer there. I never got a chance to utter one word, and I was fuming. I threw my iPhone smack into the wall! That shit shattered like my heart! All I could think about is how I let Tyesha walk out my mother's apartment unharmed, because she was pregnant! It's a decision I was now regretting!

"ARGHHHHH THAT BITCH!!! TYESHA I'M GOING TO DESTROY YOU!!!" I screamed to the top of my lungs.

PART TWO IS NOW AVAILABLE

ACKNOWLEDGEMENT

I want to thank God first and foremost. I am nothing without him. I would like to give special recognition to my wonderful husband Jai, my five beautiful children, and my handsome grandson.

Shout out to my sister Sylvia, my cousin Jeanetta aka OG Shug, and my bestie Natasha. These three are ALWAYS HUSTLING extra hard to help promote my work.

I want to thank Mr. Shameek Speight, for giving me my first platform as a writer, and being super supportive of my new career as an Indie Author. I'm overjoyed for my new beginnings, and I can't wait to pave my way into literacy history.

Yours Truly,
Lady Legacy

ABOUT THE AUTHOR

Author Lady Legacy

About The Author AUTHOR LADY LEGACY Lady Legacy was born and raised in Alabama; however, she's been a resident of Georgia since 2008. Lady Legacy is a proud wife, mother of five, and a grandmother.

As a child, she's always been interested in writing. At eleven years old, she often used poems to express her deep feelings. Over the years, her love for reading and writing, continued to manifest.

On October 7th, 2013; she started a Facebook book reading group called, "Let's Share Urban Fiction." January 2014, she became Facebook administrator for True Glory Publications. Shortly after becoming a Facebook administrator, she became a Blog Talk Radio Host, under the pen name Miko Minaj.

Encouraged by Shameek, and her sister Monique to write a book; she decided to take their advice. She started to write her first book series, signing with True Glory Publications 2017.

Paving her way into the literary world she released her first book series, 'SCANDALOUS AFFAIRS.' The first installment debut July 2017, and since then has hit #1 on Amazon's bestsellers list.

As of September 7th, 2020; National Bestselling Author Lady Legacy contract ended on good terms, with True Glory Publications, with all book rights returned to her.

Excited on her new Indie Author transition, she is currently rereleasing ten book titles, as she continues to work on releasing new book material, under her self-publishing company, Lady Legacy Presents.

BOOKS BY THIS AUTHOR

Scandalous Affairs 1

Scandalous Affairs 2

Scandalous Affairs 3

Chase A Check Never Chase A Chick 1

Chase A Check Never Chase A Chick 2

Chase A Check Never Chase A Chick 3

Kandy Kane Addickion 1

Kandy Kane Addickion 2

Kandy Kane Addickion 3

Draya & Drake

Cheat Once, Pay Twice

Made in the USA
Coppell, TX
07 January 2023

10431863R00046